The Ye... ...ne Hobby

Molly Burkett
November 30th 2008

Sburkett

By

Seth & Molly Burkett

First published by Barny Books

ISBN No: 978.1.903172.86.5

Publishers: Barny Books
                 Hough on the Hill
                 Grantham
                 Lincolnshire
                 NG32 2BB

                 Tel: 01400 250246
                 www.barnybooks.biz

I was fed up.

We'd said we'd meet up on the playing field and the others hadn't turned up, none of them. It had been my turn to take the ball and I kicked it around waiting for them to come. There wasn't a soul in sight. I sat in the goal and thought about things for a while. There wasn't much point in going home. Sophie had her friends in and you know what a lot of girls are like when they get together, giggle, giggle, giggle and not a sensible word between them.

In the end, I went off to see where my mates were. George and Greg's mother answered the door. I think she was expecting somebody else. She was wearing a swimming costume, a bikini and a sort of dressing gown over it. She looked over my head and said that the boys were down at the cricket field and why didn't I go and join them but I didn't want to go and play cricket, not the way they played it. I wanted to play football. There was nobody in at Dean's house. The neighbour leaned over the fence and said they'd all gone to London for the day. Dean's neighbour always knew more about his family than they knew about themselves. She told me which train they had gone on and when they were due back and I think she would have told me a lot more beside if I hadn't managed to mutter something about my mother expecting me home and making an escape. I could smell cooking as soon as I opened the gate when I went to David's house – sausage rolls. David's mother makes the best sausage rolls in the world, jam tarts and apple pies too. I always like calling in there when she's having a cooking session. His mother flung the door back when I knocked at their house and it was obvious that I'd walked into a situation.

No, he wasn't coming out, she told me, not until he'd apologised. He'd knocked over her flower arrangement and broken the vase.

'Christ,' I thought, 'they must have been important flowers if they make her go red in the face like that.'

David was sitting on the settee. I could see him through the door. He had his lips closed tight like the way he goes when he gets stubborn.

"Say you're sorry and come on out," I urged him.

"Why should I?" he said. "I didn't kick them over on purpose."

"That flower vase was a special one. It was a present from your Grandmother before she died."

It would finish up with them both bursting into tears and hugging each other. It always did in their house. I was best out of it so I tucked the ball under my arm and went home. I fetched my bike out of the garage and shouted out to Mum that I was going for a bike ride.

"Where are you going?" she shouted back but I didn't answer. I didn't know where I was going. I felt sorry for myself stuck on my own. The others should have let me know if they weren't coming out. Stuff them for a start.

It's funny how things just seem to happen. I didn't realise then that that one quick decision was going to make such a difference to my life. I was cycling along without any thought of where I was going. I'd nearly reached the main road that we took when we went to see Charles and I decided, on the spur of the moment, that I'd go and see him.

Charles is my Godfather. He's a gamekeeper on a big estate and you couldn't mistake him for anything else. He'd been in the army before he took up game keeping and you can see it in the way he walks head up, shoulders straight and off he goes, a bit bandy round the knees but when you see him marching off to feed his pheasants, you could easily imagine him in his number ones marching off to guard the Queen. Charles is short. He only comes up to my Dad's shoulder but he's tough. He got into a fight with three poachers one night and he was the only one standing up at the end of it. He's quite different when he's dealing with his pheasants and partridges though. He's really gentle

4

and caring then. His knowledge of the countryside and the creatures that live in it is phenomenal. I love it when we visit and walk round the estate with him.

It was a good job I hadn't told my mother where I was going. I had to cycle down the main road and its busy. It's not only that. When you start on the hill going down from Four Marks, it's difficult to slow down and there's a bend at the bottom. Cars whizz by and they seem to create a draught which pulls you along too and makes you go faster than you want to. She would have pulled her hair out if she'd known I was cycling down Four Marks hill.

Charles and Judy's cottage was about a mile down a bumpy track and Charles was setting out on his rounds when I arrived. You couldn't have mistaken him for anything else except a gamekeeper with his green tweed plus fours, hacking jacket, deer stalker hat and his three black labradors at his heel with his keeper's bag slung across his shoulder. He looked up when he saw me coming and waited for me to reach him.

"Does your mother know you've come?" he greeted me and before I could even answer, he said, "Better go in and phone to tell her you're here."

I opened my mouth to answer him. I could have phoned her on my mobile but then I thought I'd better do what Charles said. You always do when he uses that tone of voice. He had been a sergeant when he was in the army so I suppose he was used to giving orders.

I thought I was in for it and Mum would have told me off but she didn't. She said I was to phone her up when I was ready to go home and she would come and pick me up.

"That's fine," Charles said, "I'm going down the ride. I reckon I heard a carrion crow down there and I want to see if I can find its nest."

I think he was pleased to have me along with him and he chattered away as we walked along beside the river. I didn't really hear what he was saying at first. I would have

5

much rather been playing football with my mates and I was still feeling annoyed with them for letting me down. Gradually Charles' voice penetrated my thoughts and I started to listen to him. I suppose that when you're working on your own all day, it's nice to have someone to talk to and Charles started talking before we even started walking.

Charles' knowledge about wildlife is phenomenal. Although he loves the animals and birds that survive on the estate, he has a thing about carrion crows. He hates them. Enemy number one he calls them. He can't stand them ever since he found one of them pecking the eyes out of a new born lamb. He wouldn't harm a rook. He reckons they do more good than harm but a carrion crow gets him into his boots and out with his gun before you can get your coat on.

"Clarence tells me a pair nested down the ride last year but I'll put a shot up their backsides if they think they're coming back."

Charles' eyes glinted and his lips tightened at the thought of crows nesting on his patch. That wouldn't have happened if he'd been fit but he had had measles the previous year and it had taken him a long time to get over it. Clarence, the other keeper on the beat had covered Charles' patch as well as his own.

"Crows are spiteful birds and they can do a lot of damage in the rearing pens. They're loners. What we're looking for is a nest on its own. They'll build close to the trunk and high up too where they can get a good view. You won't mistake their nest for any other, it's not over tidy, not as bad as a magpie's nest mind you. Their nests are such a mess, it makes you wonder how they hold together. They're cunning are magpies. They hide their nests so well that you have the devil's own job finding them. Build lids on top of their nests and all to protect the fledglings.

They're all nasty natured birds but the carrion crow's the worst."

Charles paused for breath and thought about them for a bit.

"Rooks are alright, the clowns of the bird world are rooks. Do you know there are some people that live in the country and can't tell the difference between a rook and a crow. Can't tell an ash from an oak either."

I didn't like to interrupt him and tell him that I wasn't too sure myself.

"They're real creatures of habit are rooks. You can set your clock by them. When I first started working here, we used to shoot the young rooks, the branchers, at the beginning of May and send them up to the big house. They always ate rook pie on May the 6th and delicious it was too but they don't shoot them now. There aren't so many hungry mouths to feed. They reckon as how that nursery rhyme comes from rook pie. You know the one I mean."

"Sing a song of Sixpence," I suggested.

"That's the one." He paused for a while. "There's a lot of superstition about rooks. They say that when a land owner loses his rookery, he loses his wealth. That's what happened to the estate up yonder. He had the spinney cut down where the rooks nested and he'd had to sell up and get out before the next spring."

It was funny. I'd been round his beat with him more times than I could count. Generally, Mum and Dad and Sophie were there as well. Charles always prattled on like that about country life as it used to be and the plants and animals that dominated his world. We used to say yes and no and not really take a lot of notice but, this time, I was on my own so perhaps I was listening more carefully and wanted to know more. I didn't know an ash from an oak. I knew bumble bees were different to honey bees but I didn't know there were twenty five species of them. But I learned a lot more about them as I walked through the estate with Charles that afternoon.

Although he had spent the first half mile declaring his planned treatment of the carrion crows, Charles didn't seem in any hurry to get to the ride where he thought he had heard them. He kept stopping to point out certain things, the spot where orchids grew and the tree where the tawny owns were nesting. At one time all this talk about wildlife would have irritated me. I didn't have any great interest in tawny owls or anything like them. Football and sport were my main interests. Perhaps it was because I was walking round with Charles on my own instead of with the rest of the family that made a difference but Charles' words were sinking into my mind and his fascination with the area through which we were walking began to transfer themselves to me.

"Mind you," he was saying, "nobody could call it a nest. Tawny owls find a fairly flat place in a tree like where a branch meets a trunk and they lay their eggs there. They might put a few twigs or some moss there first but they don't always bother. It's no wonder that so many of their chicks keep falling out but they're best left alone. Even at that age, they know where they've come from and they'll clamber up the trunk faster than a mountaineer can scale a ten meter cliff."

We'd turned into the ride then, the main fire break cut through the wood like a narrow lane but wide enough to prevent flames crossing from one side of the ride to the other if ever there was a fire in the woods. It was one of my favourite places, a typical example of all that is beautiful in the British countryside. It was so quiet and peaceful, even the noise from the main road didn't penetrate the curtain of trees and the call of the rooks sank into the distance. Charles was quiet and, for a few seconds, we experienced the cathedral silence and delicate beauty of the wood. Then, with a raucous call that startled the silence, a big, black bird

8

flew across our line of vision and, without seeming to pause to aim, Charles had lifted his four bore and fired. Immediately the silence and peace of the forest had gone. The echo of the shot reverberated around the stunned forest. The startled flight of wood pigeons clapped their disapproval and a disturbed deer rustled through the undergrowth.

"Bloody crow," Charles grumbled. I had hardly ever heard him swear before, Not since he'd been one of the three Kings in the nativity play and tripped over the altar step and fallen flat on his face. "It's nesting round here somewhere but I'll get it. I'll be back with a cage trap and I'll…"

He stopped in mid sentence, his head cocked to one side. He had obviously heard something and his hunter's instinct had immediately surfaced. I listened but all I could hear was the sounds of the woodland and feel the silence returning like a summer mist rolling slowly along the ground. Then I heard a distant screaming, a sound, a scream that pierced the sky.

I looked up. There was a smudge above us, a small cloud moving swiftly across the summer sky, a wisp of smoke being tossed in the wind. It constantly changed its shape as it advanced across the sky, stretching out like a fringe, then consolidating into a moving bunch coming steadily in our direction and it was from this that the screams came.

"Swifts," Charles said shortly, "the last of the summer birds to arrive. You know summer's here when the swifts come."

Then he started to tell me all about swifts, how, when they leave the nest, they spend the rest of their lives in the air, only landing to nest and how, if they do land, they can't take to the air again because their legs are partly in their bodies and are not long enough to give them the lift they need to become airborne.

I didn't like to remind him that I knew quite a bit about swifts myself. Mum and Dad run a wildlife rehabilitation centre and we always have swifts brought in every summer. People tell us all sorts of stories about them when they bring them in, that they've lost their legs or both of them are broken when they really don't understand their life style. Few people identify them when they're on the ground. We once had a phone call from a man who said that he'd found a Sea Eagle on the beach. Mum asked him if he was sure it was a Sea Eagle. You don't generally find Sea Eagles on Skegness beach but he was adamant. He had found a Sea Eagle and he was going to bring it straight up. Two hours later, a man came walking down the hill carrying a shoe box. It would have been some Sea Eagle to be in a box that size. When Mum told him it contained a swift, he wouldn't have it but insisted it was a Sea Eagle. As soon as he had gone, she climbed over the style to the field and let it go. It was a bit embarrassing when he returned a couple of hours later with a T.V. crew to film this rare bird.

I couldn't take my eyes off those birds above us. I was fascinated by the way they were twisting and turning as one group, each of them moving at the same time as if they were glued together and they were calling as they flew, a high pitched call that sounded like a haunting scream.

"There's something upsetting them," Charles said, "they don't generally fly bunched up like that."

"One of them's bigger than the others," I said.

Charles stopped talking straight away and shaded his eyes against the sun as he looked up.

"Good God," he exclaimed, "it's a hobby," and there was a kind of wonder in his voice as he carried on giving me a mini lecture.

"They over winter in Africa you know and migrate to Europe in the summer and have their young here. They're bonny little birds but there aren't that many of them that visit hereabouts. He could have flown in with the swifts. My, look at him, Seth, look," and the wonder in his voice had changed to excitement, "He's hunting them. Look at the way he's herding them."

It seemed more like the hobby was playing with them, swinging round and in front of the screaming swifts, turning them towards the east, swooping beneath them, then soaring above them. The huddled group of birds twisted and turned trying to fly away from the dark, menacing shadow. The hobby flew high in the air until he was little more than a dot in the clear sky and then it dived. It tore into the centre of the flock so that it exploded into a hundred fragments that speckled the sky before they gathered together again, like slivers of metal being drawn into a magnet and flew on at the same steady speed.

The hobby flew alone grasping a swift in his talons and, while we watched, he started to pluck his prey and the feathers he pulled and discarded floated down like the petals of apple blossom falling on a windy day. The hobby remained in the sky above us plucking and devouring the bird that, seconds before, had been a living creature.

There was something hypnotic about the scene and I couldn't take my eyes off the small falcon. Then it shook its feathers, roused and shut its wings close to its body and dived. I'd never seen anything like it and I don't think Charles had either. As it reached the tree-tops, it spread its wings as if it was going to hover and dropped out of sight.

"It's landed in the woods," I stated.

Charles didn't say anything, not straight away. He stood there looking at the spot where the hobby had disappeared. Then he said, "I've never seen a hobby, not on this estate. I've only ever seen a stuffed one. I read how they fly so fast that they can catch a swift and eat it on the wing but I don't know anyone else who has ever seen it," and there was a kind of wonder in his voice as he spoke.

11

"Now look Seth," he said, "they're rare and they want to be left alone, so don't tell anyone what we've seen, not a word to anyone, O.K?"

"Can't I tell Mum and Dad?" I asked.

"Yes," he said, "but not another soul."

* * * *

Mum hadn't waited for me to phone and say I was ready to go home. She was sitting in the kitchen having a cup of tea with Judy. She was in a hurry to get home. She's always in a hurry. It wasn't until we were on the way home that she brought up the subject of my cycling along the main road. I knew she would. She wasn't cross though but she didn't want me going down Four Marks Hill again, not on my own. She said that it wasn't only the traffic that worried her but it was the peculiar people you get about nowadays. I knew all about that. We'd had a discussion at school about the wierdos and druggies that we might meet but I let Mum tell me anyway. She said if I went down to see Charles again she'd like me to go round by Bentworth and cut across country so I said I would even though it was a longer way round but I was thinking that I could look after myself and, although I told her I would go through the villages, sticking to the promise might be another matter.

I slept in a bit the next morning. Mum's shrill voice shouting up the stairs woke me up, in fact, I wouldn't be surprised if it woke half the village up as well. When I got dreamily out of bed and drew back the curtains I saw David stretched out on our front lawn.

"Did you say you're sorry, then?" I called down.

"Sort of," he said. "You coming out for a game?"

"Haven't had my breakfast yet."

"Bring it with you. The others are over on the field but you've got the ball."

I had half a mind not to go after the way they'd let me down the day before but I enjoyed getting out with my mates so I said I wouldn't be a minute. We played football in the morning and went fishing in the afternoon. We had to take it in turns because we only had one rod between the five of us so we finished up sitting on the bank talking. There were swallows flying low over the water. They reminded me of the swifts I had seen the day before and, instinctively, I looked up. Swifts were flying like dark arrows high in the sky. I searched the air above them, looking to see if there was another bird that looked like a big swift and I knew, in that instant, that I wanted to see the hobby again. I saw again, in my mind's eye, the scene that I had witnessed the day before, the worried knot of swifts exploding across the sky and the hobby left there, flying alone.

It was a couple of weeks before we next went down to see Charles and Judy. We called round there on the way back from seeing my grand parents. The first thing we saw when we went through the door was Charles sitting in a chair with his foot resting on a stool. He looked pale and sorry for himself. Before we could ask him what was the matter, Judy started telling us.

"Twenty-five years we've lived in this house," she started, "twenty-five years and he has to wait until I've gone out for the day to fall down the stairs and break his ankle."

Charles gave an angry grunt. He did not look happy.

Dad asked him if there was anything we could do to help. It was the busy time of the year for Charles, getting the pheasants and partridges out and setting traps for the vermin but Charles said there was no need. Young Clarence was seeing to everything.

Clarence was the other keeper on the estate and Charles always called him Young Clarence although he was older than he was. We liked Clarence although he never had much to say, in fact he hardly ever spoke at all but he smiled a lot.

"He never started to talk until he was six and he hasn't caught up yet," Charles used to say.

Clarence and his brother lived next door to Charles and Judy in a cottage that looked identical to theirs on the outside but it couldn't have been more different indoors. Clarence's brother was a long distance lorry driver and he was always picking up bargains. Their house was full of bargains from the exercise bike that was wedged in the far corner of the kitchen to the set of kettle drums that he had found in a skip in Soho.

"Never have a cup of tea with Clarry," Charles used to say. "He makes a tea bag last for weeks, just adds another from time to time and only cleans the tea pot out when there's more tea bags than liquid in it and his stew's no better. He makes that last a month, keeps adding things as he comes across them and only cleans the pot out when the solids start sticking to the bottom. Never let him cut your hair either. He trimmed mine up once and I ended up looking like I had a map of Japan on the top of my head."

"Is that why you always wear your hat indoors?" Sophie asked.

"That's part of it, girl," Charles said, "that's part of it."

"Do you wear your hat in bed as well?" Sophie wanted to know.

"No, I take it off then," Charles told her. "It's Judy's turn to wear it at night."

"Shall we have a look round for you like always?" I interrupted..

"That would be a great help, that would, lad," he said. "Your aunt takes me round in the truck but she won't go over the bumps so we're a bit limited."

"Too right, I won't, not when the bumps you point out land us in the bottom of a ditch and I have to walk four miles to the farm to get a tractor to come and pull us out."

14

Charles wasn't listening to her. He signalled me over and whispered, "Look out for them crows, boy, I don't like they varmits. See if you can find their nest. They like an old fir tree where they be well hidden," and he set about giving me instructions about where they had nested the previous year.

Sophie and I set off. Mum came part of the way with us but she turned back when the ground got marshy because she had her decent shoes on. Sophie and I went down a ride and I told her what Charles had said. We found the fir tree that Charles had described and we stood under it and looked up into the branches. It was a big, old tree and we couldn't see very far up into it.

"Give me a leg up." I said, "I'm going to see if there's a nest up there."

"You know what Mum says about you climbing trees. What's going to happen if you break your elbow again?"

"Well she won't know if you don't tell her."

It was an easy tree to climb. The branches extended from the trunk in patterns of four, two of them slightly higher than the matching two as if nature had provided a ladder for me to climb. It seemed only seconds before my head broke through the top branches only I was now moving much more cautiously. The trunk was little more than new growth at that point and it was swaying with my weight. I gingerly climbed down a couple of branches and that was when I saw the nest. I don't know how I could have missed it on the way up. It was big enough, but, when I climbed down, I realised how well camouflaged it was from underneath. As my eyes grew level with it, I was gazing at the dark eyes of a bird that was settled in it and that bird was not a crow. I didn't know what it was but it wasn't any sort of bird that I had ever seen before. I stayed in that position staring at it, not daring to move and it looked right back at me. My presence didn't seem to worry it at all. It watched me in such a way to suggest that it

15

trusted me. I couldn't see it clearly because it was well settled in the nest. I thought it was about pigeon size and the colouring on its head was so distinctive, glossy black on each side of its beak and a white collar. But it was the look in its eyes that captivated me. I am sure the bird understood that I would not harm it.

That was when Sophie started to shout wanting to know if I was alright and I couldn't answer her because I didn't want to disturb the bird. Then she started going ballistic and banging the tree trunk. She was losing her temper because I wasn't answering her. It was time I moved anyway. I eased my foot on to a lower branch and, as I transferred my weight on to it, a twig snapped off. The noise startled the bird. With a flutter of wings, it flew off and I was able to see a single egg nestled in the downy softness of the nest.

"Did you see that?" Sophie demanded as I lowered myself to the ground. "A peregrine flew out of the tree."

And then it dawned on me.

"That wasn't a peregrine," I said. "That was a hobby."

* * * *

I cycled down to the wood the following weekend. I didn't tell my mother I was going. I didn't tell anybody. I didn't call in at Charlie's cottage but I cycled right past it and along the track and I soon knew what Judy meant about it being bumpy. It was easier to push my bike along the ride where the grass was longer and the undergrowth caught in the spokes of my wheels. That was when the silence hit me and it hit me like a blow to my face. It was as if I had to push myself through a brick wall and there was nothing there. It was approaching mid-day, the time when even the song birds fell silent. There wasn't a sound. Everything was so still and quiet and I felt suddenly alone. The rat-tat of a green woodpecker's drumming broke the silence and the warning call of a blackbird heralded the familiar sounds of the woodland.

I leaned my bike against the trunk of the fir tree and looked up. There wasn't any sign of the nest or the hobby. It took me about ten attempts to get up to the lowest branch. I had to wedge my bike against the trunk and balance on that. From then on, it was easy. I climbed up very carefully as I approached the branch on which the nest was built and, once again, the feeling of being on my own surprised me. When I thought about it afterwards, I suppose I should have expected to feel a bit strange. I'd never been off on my own before. I always went to places with my mates or the family but this time, I had wanted to be on my own. I wanted to find out about the hobbies for myself only I hadn't thought that coming down to these woods which I knew so well would be so quiet and so lonely on my own. Then I thought of the last time I had climbed that tree and had nearly fallen and the thought that if I did fall, there wouldn't be Sophie at the bottom of the tree waiting for me. There wouldn't be anyone. Nobody would know where I was. A feeling of panic filled me. I took a deep breath and climbed up those last few branches.

I lifted my head above the rim of the nest and there was the same pair of dark, trusting eyes looking at me but the bird was unsettled. She spread her wings across the nest. Then, with a flurry of feathers, she flew off and I found myself looking down on three eggs nestled in the bottom of the old crow's nest. The hobby had laid two more eggs. I knew I mustn't stop her returning to the nest. It was important that once she started brooding, the eggs were kept warm. I slipped and scrambled down the tree as fast as I could. Then I lay down on the grass and gazed up, hoping to see the falcon return to her nest but the sky remained completely empty. I wondered if my presence was keeping her away so I picked up my bike and made my way back to the road.

I went round to see David when I got home, told him to come down the garden and bring a Bible with him. He brought two, said I could take one home with me, he had plenty. I didn't particularly want another Bible, I wanted him to swear on the Bible that he would keep my secret.

"Do you want us to cut our thumbs so that we swear in our blood as well like we did when Greg told us about the vicar going off with the girl from the fish and chip shop?" he asked.

"That's kid's stuff," I said, "and this is serious."

So we put the two Bibles on top of each other and David swore that he would keep my secret and I told him all about the hobby.

"Is that all?" he said. "I thought you'd done something really exciting with all this whispering and swearing on the Bible."

David didn't seem to think it was much of a secret but he promised not to tell anyone unless there was an emergency. Then we shook hands and went out to play football.

* * * *

That fir tree must have been the tallest in the wood. I know that because I fell from pretty near the top right down to the bottom of it. It was my own fault. I had sidled a bit too far along the branch to get a better view of the nest and it had snapped under my weight. It hadn't snapped right off but enough to tip me off my balance and it sent me falling. It was a funny feeling. It seemed that it was all happening in slow motion as if I was in a dream. I was lucky on two counts. One, because of the way the branches spread out from the central trunk in patterns of four, two slightly higher than the two beneath them and, secondly, because it was a pretty old tree and the needles were thick and cushioned my fall. I bounced down it rather than fell. I was

18

also lucky because of all the P.E. lessons we have at school. Some of the boys moan about Mr Carr because he takes everything so seriously and wears us out with some of the things he makes us do in the gym but, as I tumbled downwards, I was thinking of his voice shouting out, "Remember where and how you're going to land."

I knew where I was going to land alright and I only had a few seconds to think of how. The ground seemed to be coming up towards me at break neck speed but, in those few seconds, I was ready. I threw myself at the lowest branch, held on to it for a matter of seconds and dropped on to the ground.

"God," said Dave, after I'd finished telling him what it had felt like tumbling down through the branches, "I thought you were a gonner," and that's the nearest Dave ever came to swearing. His family go to Church twice on Sundays and sometimes in the week as well. They're not the sort of people to swear.

He was more shocked than I was. His face was as white as a snowfall and his hands were shaking. I felt a bit dazed as if it had all happened in a dream and wasn't real at all. Then I remembered what Dad told me about the soldiers in the war, how, when they had had a bad experience in battle, they were sent straight back into the battle zone, otherwise they would never have fought again. I looked at the fir tree and I knew I was going through a similar experience to those soldiers. The fall had shaken me up and I knew if I didn't go up that tree right away, I would never go up it again. So I asked David to give me a leg up and I was soon hoisting myself up from branch to branch and, in no time at all, I was looking down into the nest and the hen hobby was looking steadily back at me. My fall hadn't disturbed her at all. I climbed down to the ground a lot more carefully that time.

I was pleased David had come down with me that day. It was half term. My mother couldn't make out why I was getting up so early and disappearing on my bike. She usually complains that I never really stir until the afternoon so me getting up before Sophie each morning must have surprised her. I'm not that keen on getting up to go to school but this was different. I wanted to see the hobbies flying as a pair. I was sure that if I was patient enough, I would see the cock bird bringing in food for the hen in the same way that the buzzards on the other side of the wood did. I spent ages lying on the grass looking up at the sky between the branches but I neither saw nor heard the birds.

It was the Friday morning that David decided he was coming with me. He's only got one interest in life and that's football but the rest of the gang were playing cricket so he came with me instead and, as it turned out, I was pleased that he did. The fall had shaken me up more than I realised. David spent the whole journey home telling me that there was a God in heaven and that he'd been looking after me that day and he believed it. It wasn't long before he got me believing it too. I'm not into Church and that sort of thing but David said he's not into birds and that sort of thing either but that doesn't mean they don't exist. I hadn't thought about things in that way. I spent a long time lying awake in bed that night, thinking.

I cycled down to the wood on Saturday morning. I had to make a real effort to clamber up into the branches of the fir tree and wasn't I pleased that I did because, when I looked over the rim of the nest, the hobby flew off and I found myself staring down at just two eggs and a small bundle of fluff. The first hobby chick had hatched. I stood there staring at it completely mesmerised. Then a shadow flew across the sky and I knew the hen was waiting to return so I climbed reluctantly down to the ground.

I knew I should go and tell somebody about the hobbies but I didn't want to. I don't know why that bird was so important to me but it was. This hobby was special. The image of the dark, feathered arrow diving through the sky the day that I'd been out with Charles stayed in my mind. I couldn't wait to see the young hobbies fly. Something about them had really got to me. Perhaps it was the trusting way the hen had looked at me when I climbed the tree or, maybe, it was the way that the hobby had flown on that very first day. Whatever it was, those birds were important to me and they were mine. Nobody else knew they were there except Sophie of course and David but I'd sworn them to secrecy.

I got some books out of the library and read everything I could about birds of prey and hobbies in particular. There was a lot about falconry but I didn't want any falconer getting hold of one of my hobbies and walk around with it balanced on his fist. I wanted my hobbies to fly free, to soar and swoop in the sky like I had seen the adult bird flying that evening when the swifts had flown above our heads. There was a paragraph in one of the books asking people to report sightings of rare birds of prey. They had listed six birds and the hobby was one of them. That did make me think. Who should I report it to? It was difficult to say anything to Charles because he was never on his own now that he was having to sit in a chair with his foot on a stool. I wondered if there was anyone at school who would know. It wasn't any good saying anything to my mates. They were only interested in football and skate boarding. Dave knew about them but he wasn't really interested and I didn't think any of the teachers would be either. That was until I saw Mr Smithers striding down the corridor. He didn't teach me because I wasn't in his science set but I knew who he was. He was one of the first teachers you noticed when you went into assembly. He was a big man. He stood head and shoulder above everyone else in the hall. He had thick, dark hair that fell over his forehead and into his eyes when he got excited. He was a very excitable man. He was Welsh and spoke with a Welsh accent that became more and more pronounced the more he had to say. If you made a noise or

21

were late into the hall, he would turn and stare at you in a way that made you wish you could disappear through the floor. His stare was notorious throughout the school. It was the only thing that some of the students feared. They didn't muck around when Mr Smithers was there. If anyone stepped out of line when he was about or made too much noise, then the whole school would have heard what he thought about that particular person. He lapsed into a sort of lyrical Welsh on these occasions so we were never too sure what he did actually say but we knew he wasn't pleased. All we could hope was that we wouldn't be the one to be picked on. His Christian name was Rex. I knew that because the boys in Year 12 called him Sexy Rexy, not to his face mind you. There was one boy that did though. I don't think he meant to but the name slipped out and so did the boy. Mr Smithers had him by the scruff of his neck and I don't know if he carried him or if he walked out but he didn't come back. When I asked one of the boys on the bus why they called him that, he said it was because he was always talking about the birds and bees.

I came face to face with him in the corridor. I'd never spoken to him in my life and I don't know what made me think he would be interested in the hobbies but, as we came abreast of each other, I said, "Do you know anything about birds, Sir?"

He came to a halt and looked down at me with those dark, brooding eyes of his.

"Ah, Burkett," he said, "the boy with a football permanently attached to his right foot."

"Left, Sir," I said, "left. I'm left footed."

"Well, young man, I know a good deal about birds," and his voice boomed down the corridor and returned to us in an elongated echo.

"Do you know about hobbies?"

"Ah, hobbies, the masters of the skies, one of the most beautiful things in the universe."

"That's what I think, Sir," and I started telling him all about my hobbies and how I had read in this book that I should have reported them.

"Keep it to yourself, laddie," he boomed and his words echoed along the corridor and came back to us. "Keep it to yourself or you'll have all these twitcher people descending on you disturbing the birds and blocking the roads and you'll think the Third World War has broken out. You come and see me at lunchtime tomorrow and we'll work out a plan."

I nodded and smiled. I felt sort of relieved for sharing my secret.

"Oh, and Burkett," His voice boomed down the corridor.

"Yes Sir?"

"Tuck in your shirt."

It turned out that Mr Smithers was a big bird man. He asked me if he could come and see the hobbies when they started to fly. I couldn't believe that a teacher would ask my permission for something like that. I told him that I would have to ask Charles and told him who Charles was and he said that he would be delighted to meet him. I wasn't so sure that Charles would want to meet him. They were both sort of loners.

As it was, we went down to Charles' cottage a couple of days later. Mum had had a kingfisher that had broken its wing. Dad had taken one look at it and told her that she didn't have a cat in hell's chance of keeping it alive. Kingfishers would only eat live food.

"We'll see," Mum had said and, from then on, she had tried all kinds of tricks to try and make the anchovies she bought from the fishmonger look as though they were swimming but, in the end, she had to resort to going down the stream and catching tiddlers. And the kingfisher thrived. And its wing mended. Then, without warning, it was dashing at the wire on its cage trying to escape. It was ready to go. It's no use delaying their release because they can start to decline if you do, so Mum put the bird in a box and announced that we were going down to Charles. She left a note for Dad to say where we were going. Sophie and I climbed in the back and we were off.

Charles had had his plaster off and was hobbling around with the aid of the stick. He drew me to one side when Judy, Sophie and Mum were setting off for the lake. We knew they would be gone an age. It's not the actual releasing that takes the time, it's the watching to make sure the animal can cope in its new environment that stretches your patience. Then Mum and Judy would want to gossip. They always did. They had a love of gossiping and Sophie and I used to get fed up waiting around for them to finish.

"Pity you can't drive, boy," he said. "you could have driven me down the wood."

"I don't mind trying," I told him but he shook his head.

"Don't know where Judy's hidden the key. We'll have to use the bike. Young Clarry's been calling and he tells me as how those crows are back and he reckons they're nesting up in that big old fir tree up the main ride. He said as how, if you stood back, you could see a bit of a nest. Well I'm getting up there and I'm putting a shot right through that nest. I'll put paid to them there vermin, that I will."

That was when I told him about the hobbies. Well I had to. He could have shot up through the nest and killed them. I couldn't let that happen.

I don't think Charles believed me at first. Then he wanted to go and see for himself and urged me to get his bike out. The bike was in the shed alright but I doubt if it had seen the light of day for the last ten years. It took a bit of time to disentangle it from the wire and debris that had been dumped on top of it. I had pumped up the tyres for a start and, to my surprise, they stayed up. I pushed the bike out to where Charles was waiting and it was hard work.

The brakes were hard on and the chain squeaked but some generous use of the oil can eased that. I helped Charles up on to the saddle and he was away, turning the pedals with his one good foot and holding the other straight in front of him. He held the handlebars with one hand and used the other to wave his walking stick. I wasn't surprised when he careered down the slope and landed in a heap at the bottom. We reorganised ourselves. I took hold of the handle bars and started pushing the old sit up and beg type bike through knee high grass while Charles sat back and told me all that he would like to do to people who stole his pheasants.

We turned into the ride and I stopped so suddenly that Charles lurched forward and took hold of the handle bars to keep his balance. I was looking at the ruts in the ground and wondering how I was going to get Charles and the bike over them when I heard him exclaim. I looked up and there were the two hobbies, both of them, and they were flying as I had never seen birds fly before. It was almost as if they were dancing. They were so graceful. The two of us stood there and watched all the perfections of an aerial ballet, darting and soaring, diving and hovering, a perfection of beauty and power.

"They're hawking insects," Charles stated.

That is just what they were doing, taking insects in mid flight and returning from time to time to the tree in which the nest was situated.

"They hunt a lot of insects when they have young," Charles said. "There's more calcium in insects and young birds need that to make sure they grow strong bones."

I knew that anyway but I let Charles tell me. Mum always adds calcium to the food when she has young birds to rear and she adds extra vitamin A as well to help them absorb it.

We must have stood and watched the falcons for twenty minutes or more. Then they lifted over the trees, flying one slightly behind the other, flying together almost as if they were fastened to one another and disappeared. We waited there for a long time but we didn't see them return to the nest. Charlie thought they would be hunting along another ride.

We stood under the fir tree for a long time. Charles stared up at the nest muttering under his breath.

"That's an old crow nest alright. Don't know how I've missed it. I'd have put a shot through that if I'd known it was there," and he sounded as if he really meant it like he was still in the war and preparing for an attack on the enemy.

Then he turned to me and said in his normal voice, "Hobbies like to nest in old crow's nests. They're built sturdy and it saves them taking time to build their own. I'd like to get up there and see if all of those three eggs have hatched but Judy would never talk to me again if I broke anything else."

So I climbed the tree. The old bike of his wasn't a lot of good for cycling but it was as firm as a rock when I wedged it against the tree trunk and used it as a step to reach the lowest branch. From then on, it was easy going. I was used to it and I knew where all the good footholds were. It took me no time at all to draw level with the nest. I didn't expect to see the adult birds. I thought they would still be flying so I was startled when my head drew level with the nest and there was a flurry of wings as the hen took off. I automatically went to step back and I nearly lost my balance. I had to take hold of a branch to steady myself and, of course, it was the branch on which the nest was built. I thought for a second that I had tipped the whole thing over but it held firm. I was just thankful that crows do build strong nests. I clambered up to the next branch and sure enough there were two chicks nestled in the centre of the nest, one looking bigger than the other. I guessed the smaller one hadn't been hatched long, in fact, it still had the egg tooth that birds use to cut their way out of the shell on

26

the bridge of its beak. The two chicks looked great with pale blue eyes and a mass of grey white down. I fought down the temptation to pick them up and hold them. The third egg lay to one side. I wondered about taking it as a kind of memento but Charles was getting impatient and calling out to know what I was doing. His voice echoed round the tree tops, so I slithered back down to the ground.

Charles was really pleased when I told him that two of the eggs had hatched. He'd never seen hobbies on his beat before, never thought about them nesting on his patch. He said that there was still time for the third egg to hatch. The hens didn't lay their eggs all at the same time. They generally laid an egg every other day and sometimes they missed out altogether and there was a longer gap. The young hatched out at the same interval. I knew that of course but I let Charles tell me all over again. He explained exactly how the chick developed and how the parent bird can hear it chirping inside the egg as it approaches maturity. Charles likes telling you things like that. Then he said we'd better go and tell Clarry about the hobbies.

Clarry and his brother were having a cup of tea. It looked more like black syrup to me. They invited us to sit down and have a cup with them. We sat down but neither of us wanted a cup of tea. It wasn't too comfortable sitting in their house. The brothers had made most of their own furniture and they weren't very good at cutting legs to the same length. I kept slipping forward on my chair and I noticed that Charles was sitting on the edge of his.

Clarry's brother, the long distance lorry driver, had a week's conversation bottled up inside him. Now that he had two of us caught in his net, so to speak, he started on a speech without a full stop. Charles found it difficult to find a gap where he could break in and tell Clarry about the hobbies.

"I knowed all about they," Clarry said when Charles managed to interrupt the non stop monologue. "I been watching they."

"Why in the devil didn't you tell me?" Charles demanded.

"He'd tell you all in his own good time," Albert spoke for his brother. "Now would you have a dish of rabbit stew," he asked, "we've just warmed it up."

We both shook our heads. It smelt good but I'd seen what it looked like when he had lifted the lid and stirred it round a bit.

It was when we returned to the cottage with Charles balancing on the bike and using a good deal of bad language about Clarry not telling him about the hobbies, that I told him about Mr Smithers and the bit in the book about having to report the hobbies to the authorities and how Mr Smithers had told me not to bother.

"He sounds like a man with a bit of sense," Charles said. "You tell him to come and see me."

I wished that I'd never told that Sexy Rexy about the hobbies or told him that Charles would be pleased to meet him. It was only three days later when I cycled down to the woods after school. As I went down the drove, I could hear his voice booming out like a fog horn. There were the two of them sitting out in the garden with a bottle of Charlie's home made wine between them and, judging by the amount left in the bottle, they'd been there for a long time. They were so busy laughing and talking that it was some time before they noticed me standing there. Charles saw me first and he said I'd timed things just right because he was about to show Rex round his beat.

"Leave your bike there and jump in the car," Mr Smithers told me. I told him I preferred to go on my bike. "Go on," he said, "we might be gone for ages."

We were.

Charlie wanted to show Rex everything, even where he'd put his foot down a rabbit hole and sprained his ankle and Rex wanted to know all sorts of things that didn't seem very important to me.

He had a little two door Mini and I'd had to clamber over the front seat and find room to sit down amongst old boots, jumpers, walking sticks, maps and all the other clutter. Mr Smithers had to kind of fold himself up to get into the driving seat so that his knees hovered above his elbows. I'd never been so uncomfortable in my life. I don't know if it was the ruts in the ground or Mr Smither's inability to drive the car in a straight line. By the time Charles had shown him his new pheasant pens and the lake where Mum had released the kingfisher and the tree where the buzzards were nesting, it was getting late. We reached the fir tree where the hobbies were nesting as the pink glow towards the horizon told us that sunset was approaching. The two men leaned against the car and discussed all manner of things while I gazed at the sky and hoped to catch a glimpse of the small falcons.

Then Charles suggested that I could climb up and see if the third egg had hatched. Rex bent over and I climbed on to his back. It was sturdier than the bike. I clambered up through the branches. I could hear the voices of the two men droning on and on but I suppose the pine needles dulled the sound because they seemed to be a long way away. I had the world to myself up amongst the branches. It was a comfortable world and I felt content. The nest was shaded from the fading sunlight but I could see the two fledglings clearly, the elder of the two standing firmly while the younger one, seeming to be unaware of my presence, shook his half grown feathers and a miniature cloud of dust blew up in my face and made me want to sneeze. I couldn't see the egg so I carefully eased my hand over the edge to pick it up. That was when I touched something damp. Climbing on to a higher branch, I looked

29

down into the nest. I could see the egg then or what was left of it. It was rocking from side to side and the emerging chick was restrained by the merest belt of shell and, as that broke, there was a chattering in the sky above me and I knew the parent birds were close by.

I couldn't believe my luck. Every time I saw the hobbies fly, I was filled with the wonder of their mastery of the air. Finding the nest had strengthened that feeling of wonder but to actually see one of the birds hatching was a moment that nobody could share. The damp chick in the bottom of the nest looked tiny beside the two fledglings. The middle one of the three was at least five days old to my knowledge but I couldn't stay there staring at it. The hen needed to return to the nest and me to the ground.

The two men were still sitting at the bottom of the tree. I chose my moment to tell them that the third egg had hatched. Charles used that as an excuse to explain to us, yet again, how chicks develop in the egg.

It was getting dark by the time we got back to the cottage. Judy came out of the house to say that Mum was on the phone wanting to know where I was. Before I could answer, Mr Smithers had picked up my bike, hoisted it on to the car roof and said, "That's alright. Tell her I'm bringing him home."

I started to tell him that I'd be alright on my bike but he didn't listen. He had fetched a load of rope out of the boot which he and Charles started to untangle. I could have been half way home before they got it sorted out. Then they started to tie the bike on by wrapping the rope round and round the roof and the bike together, passing it through one car door to the other then over the top of the roof. Charles stood at one door and Sexy Rexy at the other and every time they passed the rope on, they would call, "Over to you." This seemed to amuse them no end and by the time they had used up all the rope, they were giggling like a couple of girls. They sounded just like Sophie and her friends when she has them home for a sleep over.

Then we set off for home but it wasn't that easy. My door wouldn't shut, neither would the driver's door, not with all that rope wrapped round the roof. There was such a pattern of rope woven above our heads that it felt like we were caught in a fishing net. It didn't seem to worry Mr Smithers. He pulled his door towards him and manipulated his elbow to hold it firm. He didn't seem to notice that I was having trouble keeping mine in any kind of order. It flapped backwards and forwards like washing on a clothes line. Sometimes I caught hold of it and held on to it for a while and sometimes it escaped my grasp and crashed back against the side of the car. It was a wonder it didn't break off its hinges. Rex was humming contentedly. By the time we reached Four Marks, he was singing at the top of his voice. Although I recognised some of the tunes, I didn't know the words because he was singing in Welsh.

When we reached our house, Mr Smithers was out of the door before I had disentangled myself from the end of the rope that had been steadily wrapping itself round my seat. He said that he would explain the situation to my parents and disappeared up the path. Mum was at the door looking a bit startled when I caught up with him. Knee length shorts didn't really suit him, neither did the yellow and orange striped shirt. I quickly introduced him to Mum and said that he was one of our teachers. She seemed relieved and asked him in for a drink.

"Make it coffee," I said to Dad who had come out to see what was happening, "black," and I went off to rescue my bike.

I didn't know much about drinking but I did know that Sexy Rexy had had to make three attempts to drive into our road and if he had any of Dad's home made wine, he probably wouldn't have made the corner at all on his return journey. Charles had shown Dad how to make wine and the stuff Dad made was even more lethal than the wine Charles made. 150 % proof it was, my mother used to claim. Sophie was always trying to explain to her that it couldn't possibly be 150% anything but she didn't get the message. The three of them were still sitting in the lounge talking when I went up to bed.

Mum and Dad were out seeing to the birds when we got up the next morning, so Sophie and I started organising breakfast. Mum appeared at the back door and said, "What a nice man." I didn't need to be told who she meant.

We saw a lot of Mr Smithers in the next couple of weeks. He seemed to be interested in everything. He would bring some old clothes and help clean out the aviaries and things like that. He wasn't the same person that he was at school. When I saw him there, he would walk past me as if I didn't exist. I preferred it that way. The hobbies were private. They were mine.

He spent a lot of time down with Charles and Charles was pleased with his help. His ankle had mended but it was still troubling him and he was having to rest it a good deal. Mr Smithers helped with the pheasant pens or clearing the undergrowth but most of the time, he went down to see the hobbies. He had to pass the end of our road to reach the woods and he would often call in to see if anyone wanted to go with him. Well I wanted to go down there. I was beginning to love the peace and beauty of those woods and to catch a glimpse of the hobbies was like the icing on the cake. But I didn't want to go with Mr Smithers. I wanted to go on my own. They were my birds. I had found them. If I hadn't shinned up the tree that evening Sophie and I had gone there, nobody would have known the hobbies were there. It seemed to me that Mr Smithers was taking them over. He was down there most evenings when the two adult birds put up the aerial flight that surpassed the flight of any other bird in sheer power and beauty. It wasn't only the hobbies though. He and Charles were spending a lot of time together. The two of them went to the pub in the village for a drink some evenings, mostly when Aunt Judy had locked the cupboard where Charles kept his home made wine and wouldn't let them have the key. They'd even been to a football match together. They had asked me if I wanted to go with them but I couldn't. I was playing in a match myself but I wouldn't have gone anyway. If he wasn't down at Charles, he'd be at our house giving Mum a hand with the animals.

It was my best friend Dave that started the rumours. He had called round one day when Mr Smithers was out in the stable with Mum helping to settle a badger that had been knocked over. I hadn't told any of my friends about Mr Smithers coming round. It wasn't that I didn't want them to know, I didn't think it was any of their business. They hadn't wanted to know about the hobbies, so I didn't mention that Mr Smithers had been coming down to watch them. It was a real shock when I got on the school bus the day after David had called round. Our school bus arrives at eight o'clock and I can generally manage to get there by five past. The problem is that I like my bed especially at half past seven in the morning. I've got it all worked out – throw the covers back at a quarter to eight, a quick wash and dress as I go down the stairs, grab a sandwich from the kitchen, pick up my bag and down to the bus stop. Sophie's always there first and she holds the bus up for me. I always get a welcome and it's always the same one from the bus driver: "We're supposed to leave at eight o'clock y'know." He doesn't know how to smile. The others on the bus have a bit more variety in their welcome. I just go down to my place and say good morning to everyone as I go by. Only this morning, it was different. There wasn't a sound when I reached the bus, not a single sound. Even the bus driver was staring intently at something in the road and didn't even look at me when I climbed on board. Some of the people on board looked a bit uncomfortable so I guessed there had been a bit of trouble so I started to make my way down the central aisle saying 'Good morning,' as I went.

Then one of the big boys started called out that Seth Burkett's mother was having it off with the science teacher.

I didn't know what to do. I stood in the aisle between the seats and looked at him. I was tongue tied. I looked round and there were all the other boys sitting there, grinning, with that look on their faces as if they were expecting a fight. Then one of the other lads called out something about my mother and Sexy Rexy. So I looked him straight in the face and said, "Are you sick or something," and went and sat down beside Dave. He was grinning too. I wanted to hit him but I had enough sense to realise that if I did anything at that moment, the tension could develop into a fight and I would be at the bottom of the pile.

I didn't say anything to Dave when we got off the bus. I didn't want to talk to him. It had to be him that had told them all about Mr Smithers coming round to our house. I didn't like them talking about my Mum like that. She didn't muck about with men. She wasn't that sort of person. My Mum and Dad were an item. I walked home that evening as if everything was normal but I was thinking of the boys on the bus and the looks on their faces. I didn't go and look in the cake tin when I got home. I went straight up to my bedroom and shut the door. Those boys had made me feel dirty. They thought they were being funny. Perhaps I would have laughed as well if they had been talking about somebody else's mother but they weren't. They were talking about mine.

Dad came home from work. He came upstairs after a while and knocked on my bedroom door and asked me if I was alright. I told him I was. I couldn't tell him what they had said about Mum. I wanted to be on my own for a bit.

I didn't eat a lot for supper. I wasn't hungry and that wasn't like me. Dad looked at me in a funny way and asked

34

me again if I was feeling alright. Mum wanted to know if I was being bullied at school. I almost shouted at them that I was alright. I ran upstairs and shut my bedroom door with a slam and leaned against it. I'd only been there a couple of seconds when I heard the unmistakable sound of Mr Smithers car stopping outside. I guessed he would ask me to go down to the woods with him. I knew he wanted to take a photo of the young hobbies in the nest or, rather, he wanted me to take one for him. He had told me when I saw him at school that day. But I wasn't going with him. I didn't want to see him. How could I be sure that he wasn't interested in my Mum in a sexy sort of way like the boy on the bus had suggested. Dad shouted up the stairs that Rex was downstairs and did I want to go down to the woods with him and I shouted back that I didn't. I shut my eyes and immediately a picture of the hobbies hunting along the ride came into my mind and, suddenly, I wanted to see them more than anything else in the world. They were clean and pure and uncomplicated. I shouted out that I was coming and dashed down the stairs two at a time and ran out to the purple Mini just as Mr Smithers was driving off. He leaned over the front seat and pushed the door open. I jumped in while the car was still moving. He hadn't thought about using the brake.

We didn't talk. I didn't want to say anything to him and he didn't say anything to me but I caught him looking at me sideways from time to time. We didn't call in for Charles but bumped down the ride until we were near the fir tree in which the hobbies were nesting. We walked the last hundred meters. We didn't want the birds to be frightened by the car. We still didn't talk. It wasn't so much that I didn't want to talk to Mr Smithers but I didn't know what to say to him. Perhaps he was interested in my Mum in the way that that boy had suggested. You see a lot about that sort of thing on the telly but I didn't know much about it.. Some of the boys looked at those kind of films and giggled about them but it didn't mean anything to me. I could take it or leave it or I thought I could.

Then suddenly I was running. I had seen something lying on the ground beneath the tree and I knew instinctively that one of the young hobbies was in trouble. I was sure that it would be dead. It was a long way for such a tiny thing to fall if it had fallen out of the nest. I was sure that it would be the largest of the three chicks. Its feathers were well down and Charles had thought it would be branching soon. Even as I approached, I could see a slight movement, a faint stirring of its tiny legs. It wasn't the oldest chick that had fallen, it was the youngest, the smallest of the three. The pointed feathers, still protected with the translucent sheaths, were pushing through the down but that was the only sign of growth. It was still a tiny, helpless thing lying there with its eyes closed. I knelt down beside it. I hesitated to touch it but Mr Smithers wasn't far behind me and he picked it up. I thought he was rough with it, the way he turned it upside down and pulled out its wings.

"There's no injury," he said, "it must have landed softly but there's nothing in its crop. We need to get it back in the nest as soon as possible. Can you make it with one hand?"

It wasn't easy climbing up the tree only using one hand. Mr Smithers had taken off his scarlet bobble hat and put the fledgling carefully into it and, once I had managed to climb on to the lowest branch, he had handed it up to me as if it was a piece of delicate porcelain. The two bigger chicks were in the nest, both with bulging crops. Their feathers were well down although some of those on the younger birds were still held in their protective sheaths which made them look like quills rather than feathers. I placed the smallest chick in the nest. It looked so small and helpless beside its siblings. Then I started down the tree. The red bobble hat got in the way and there wasn't room to put it in my pocket so I put it on my head. I felt stupid but it was much easier to clamber down to the ground with two free hands. As I jumped down from the last branch, Mr Smithers looked up from the ground where he was sitting with his back against a tree.

"You can keep the hat," he said, "I've half a dozen more of them at home. My cleaning lady keeps knitting them for me. I'm never sure what she expects me to do with them."

I didn't want his hat but I thought he might be offended if I refused it, so I pulled it down over my ears and went and laid on the grass near him.

"It's odd to find the bird like that. It wouldn't have climbed out of the nest on its own. It wouldn't have had the strength. The bigger one could have pushed it out when it stood on the rim or a crow or magpie could have raided the nest and lifted it. There's always the possibility that the parent birds could have thrown it out of the nest themselves because there's something wrong with it and they know it won't grow into a healthy adult. It's uncanny how wild creatures know this so early. If that's the case, they'll tip it out again so I think we'd better wait for a bit until they return to the nest and settle for the night."

So we waited. I lay on the grass and watched the sky expecting to see a dark shadow returning to the tree but it stayed empty. Mr Smithers lay there with his eyes half closed. I thought he'd fallen asleep. Then he said, "What's bothering you, Seth? Don't you like me being around? Is that it?"

"No, you're alright," I told him and he was. I had resented him at first but he fitted in and he helped Mum a lot. Then I got to thinking about Mum and I added, "I suppose you are."

"Come on, Seth," he said, "out with it," and I told him. I told him about the boys on the bus and how David who was supposed to be my best friend must have told them about him coming round to our house.

"Does it matter?" he asked.

Yes, it did matter. She was my Mum and she wasn't like that.

"Right then, we'll do something about it," he said. "I suppose you think David has let you down."

"Yes, he has. I don't know that I want to see him again."

"You will though, won't you? You're in the same class at school. You can't go on avoiding him. Perhaps he didn't realise that the older boys would carry on like that but I'm afraid a lot of them do. It makes them feel grown up and important. It's just talk. They don't really mean anything by it."

"But David was grinning like they were."

"He could have been embarrassed. A lot of people laugh or make a joke about something because they don't know how to handle a situation. How long have you been best friends with David?"

"Years and years," I mumbled.

"Well, he could be feeling as miserable as you are. Have you asked him?"

I shook my head.

"Perhaps you should. It's always best to talk things over and bring it out in the open. And Seth, I'm not having it off with your mother. I respect her too much to even think of such a thing and I'm sure she's not having it off with anyone else either. Your mother and father are very much in love. You only have to see them together to know that. Come on, we better go round and tell Charlie about the young hobby, then he can keep an eye open for it."

And that is what we did. Charlie had just opened a bottle of his parsnip wine and, of course, Sexy Rexy sat down to help him drink it. They followed that up with a drop of his dandelion and we had our usual erratic journey back to the village. I walked the last hundred meters. I told him it would save him turning round in the road but I wasn't sure that he would have made the corner.

Dave wasn't at school the next day. That was odd for a start. He always used to give me a call on his mobile when he wasn't going to make it but he didn't that day. I went round to his house when I got off the bus. He was looking at TV and his Mum was ironing. He wouldn't take his eyes off the screen as if there was something on it that he really wanted to see and it was a programme for toddlers.

"Turn it off, Dave," I said but he just grunted so I got up and turned it off for him. He still wouldn't look at me. That wasn't like Dave. We'd started infant school together and we'd been friends ever since. His Mum was chattering through the door at us but I didn't hear a word she said. I was too concerned about Dave. He looked pale and uncomfortable so I suggested we walked up the garden. We hadn't taken more than a few steps before Dave turned towards me and said, "I didn't know they were going to make stories up like that, Seth, honest," and he started to cry.

I'd never seen David cry before. I didn't know what to say but his mother opened the kitchen window and asked if we wanted something to drink.

"What was that all about?" she asked when we went indoors and David told her.

"Dirty little devils," she said. "That's why you didn't go to school today was it. You didn't know how to handle it. You're going to hear a lot worse than that before you're much older but don't you go sucking up to boys because they think they're clever using words and having ideas in their small minds. Tell them you don't like that kind of talk. They'll probably make fun of you but they'll respect you in the end. You decide what's right in life and what's wrong and you stick to it. If you remember that, you won't go far wrong."

I'd never heard Mrs Mason go on like that before. She's very quiet and religious and spends a lot of time at Church but she sounded just like my Mum that day.

Dave came round to our house and we played on the computer until we heard a car hooting outside and there was the purple Mini parked on the verge and Mr Smithers unfolding himself and climbing out of it. I started telling David about the hobby falling out of the nest and how we were going back to see if it had settled.

"Why don't you come with us?" I asked and he said he would if it was alright with his Mum.

Dave sat in the back of the Mini and I could see him bouncing up and down as we started down the track. He was very quiet which isn't like him but I think he was a bit in awe of Mr Smithers. He'd never been out with a teacher before although Sexy Rexy didn't look much like the teacher that stood at the back of the hall and watched us going into assembly. The knee length shorts, striped shirt and purple bobble hat were a bit confusing as well. Dave looked a bit dazed when we stopped in the ride and climbed out of the car.

"You can sit in the back on the way home," he announced but I hardly heard him. I had seen the fluffy, half feathered fledgling lying on the ground and I was running towards it. Mr Smithers wasn't far behind me. David followed much more slowly. Mr Smithers picked up the bird and ran his hands over it. The young hobby was much more alert than it had been the day before. Its eyes were open and it looked round at us. It didn't seem one bit concerned.

"There's nothing wrong with it," Mr Smithers said but I wasn't so sure. I had seen the other two fledglings in the nest and this bird wasn't as alert as they were and its eyes weren't as bright either.

"I think we ought to take it home for Mum to rear," I said.

I could see that Mr Smithers was uncertain.

"There's a problem about that," he said. "Hobbies will be returning to Africa in August and I doubt if she could get this one flying and hunting by then or strong enough to make the journey south. We've got to do what's best for the bird and I think it would be much better if its own parents will accept it back. I think we should give it one more chance."

He took off his purple bobble hat and gently laid the young bird in the centre of it. Handing it to me, he clasped his hands together to give me a lift up.

I climbed up carefully so that I didn't jolt the chick. I was concentrating on the climb so I was startled to hear David's voice right behind me. He had followed me up. I signalled for him to be quiet and climbed up so that I was level with the nest. So did David. You wouldn't have thought the two bigger chicks had made any movement from the day before. They were in exactly the same positions, the larger bird sitting on the rim of the nest. She was almost fully feathered and only the down on the top of her head and a small patch on her chest showed that she was not fully grown. They had obviously been fed and the crops at the base of their necks stuck out like carbuncles. I slipped the third chick back into the nest and started to descend until I saw that David hadn't moved. At first I thought he was frightened because he hadn't realised we were such a long way from the ground but he wasn't. He was staring at the chicks in the nest as if he was hypnotised. He was fascinated by them. I had to reach up and tug his trouser leg before he followed me.

"That was something," he said as he landed on the ground.

We went round to the cottage to tell Charlie about the young bird being on the ground again. He was hobbling round with a walking stick in one hand and a shillelagh in the other. He said he'd have a look along there first thing in the morning. He'd be able to drive himself now as soon as he'd found where Judy had hidden the key and he started lifting up the corner of the carpet and looking up the chimney while Judy carried on knitting. Then he saw David and wanted to know who he was so I introduced him and told Charles that David was brilliant at music and Charles said that that was funny because so was he. He felt along the mantelpiece and picked up a mouth organ and started to play it. He played some good tunes too. Sexy Rexy said that he wasn't bad on the Jew's harp and Charles said he'd got one of those too. That was on the mantelpiece as well. The two men started playing a sort of duet. Then they decided they could play the glasses as well, so Charlie lined up some glasses on the table and started tapping them with a pencil and listening to the sound it made. The tunes they thought they were playing were better without the glasses and much, much better without Mr Smither's voice chanting his Welsh hymns.

"I think we ought to be going home," I said, "David's mother is particular about him being home on time."

We got out at the corner and watched the purple Mini speeding off down the road.

"My Godfather isn't like yours," David said. "He's a curate and he sends me a Bible every Christmas and birthday. I've got thirteen."

"Charlie gave me a stuffed stoat for my birthday," I said.

"What do you do with a stuffed stoat?"

"I've got it under the bed at the moment."

"I'll swop you a Bible for it," David said.

I thought about it but decided I'd rather have the stoat.

Charles phoned up the next morning as Mum was getting ready to rush off to work and I was half way through the front door. He had picked up the body of the young falcon at the foot of the tree and wanted to know if Mum could collect it and arrange to have a post mortem done on it. I knew straight away that he was talking about the youngest hobby that I had taken back to the nest. I heard Mum say that she would go round at lunch time.

"I knew we should have brought it home. I wanted to pick it up and bring it back for you to rear," I burst out.

"Look Seth, we'll talk about it later. Hurry up and move or you'll miss the bus," but I didn't feel like hurrying. It was as if a wave of sadness had covered me. That hobby was special. I had seen it hatch and I had wanted to see it fly.

The bus was already there and Sophie was standing in the doorway shouting at me to hurry. When I did get on, they all started singing a song about someone walking so slow they started going backwards. I had to laugh. It was like a song that had been on the telly the night before but they had changed the words a bit. We carried on singing all the way to school with everyone making up their own words.

I didn't like anyone seeing me talk to Mr Smithers at school as a friend so I wrote him a note and asked the lady in the office to put it in his pigeon hole. He wrote a note back saying that he would call round that evening and if Mum hadn't arranged a post mortem, he knew someone who could help. I found the note in my shoe bag when I went down to change for P.E.

Mum had already sent the bird off. She said that she thought there was something wrong with it. She had had a good look at it and the weight on the breast was unevenly distributed and that's always a bad sign. I wasn't too sure that I wanted to go down to the woods with Mr Smithers when he called round that evening but, in the end, I did go with him and I was pleased I did because as we climbed out of the Mini, we were almost bombed by the two adult hobbies and we had to duck to get out of their way. They were flying round and round just above our heads, then they were climbing high in the sky and diving down towards us and, all the time, they were calling and the two birds at the nest were calling back at them. Mr Smithers signalled for us to go and shelter under a tree. He took out his binoculars and gazed up at the fir tree, then he handed them across to me. They were super binoculars. They made the young hobbies seem so close that I felt I could reach out and touch them. I could see the colours of their feathers. Their markings weren't as sharp as those of the adult birds. Their heads were similar and the feathers on the tops of their legs were reddy brown, like pairs of trousers. I could see that the older chick was not at the nest at all. She was branching. She kept spreading her wings and bending down so that she was almost bouncing on the branch as if she was going to take off and fly but then she would regain her balance and rouse and stay where she was. The parent birds flew so close to her that I thought they were going to push her off and, all the time, they were calling to each other. This must have gone on for twenty minutes and I was beginning to think that she never was going to fly, not that day, when she seemed to tumble off the branch and she was flying. Her flight was unbalanced and uncoordinated at first but, as she flew, it became stronger. The adult birds were urging her on. The hen started to fly away from her and the fledgling followed, calling out as if she was telling the hen to slow down. As they flew up towards the sky, they became dark shadows but it was easy to pick out the young bird because she didn't have the grace and power of her parent although, in the time that we watched her, she became stronger and we could see the beauty of her flight beginning to develop. Then all three birds were flying along the ride again and, as they came abreast of the fir tree, the young bird lifted and landed clumsily on the branch that it had left such a short time earlier.

I had seen the bird make its first flight. We leaned back against the tree trunk and I think we were both thinking of the aerial performance we had just seen. Then Mr Smithers spoilt it all by asking, "What do you think about girls?"

I didn't think anything about girls and I told him so. The girls I knew were silly and they giggled. They were always putting notes in my pencil case saying that one or other of them fancied me. Well, I didn't fancy them. I had more important things to think about.

"Only there's this girl in Year 10, Mary Pettit, do you know her? She likes anything to do with the countryside. She would love to see the hobbies flying. Would you mind if I asked her?"

Well, I did mind. I didn't want to share them with anyone else but it seemed churlish to say so.

"Alright," I said, "as long as she doesn't get in the way."

You would have thought anyone with a name like Mary Pettit would be small and pretty. Well she wasn't. She was nearly a head taller than me for a start and had a pimple on her nose. Her hair was pulled back in a pigtail and she wore glasses but she had a smiley face.

It was a couple of days later that Mr Smithers brought her with him. I heard him hooting out in the road. I was doing my homework in my bedroom and I'd nearly finished. I looked out of the window and there was the purple Mini with Mr Smithers leaning on the horn and this girl sitting on the back seat. She looked a bit odd with her nose pressed against the window. I didn't really want to go and meet this girl but I thought I'd better get it over.

Mr Smithers was in a hurry. He usually was. The engine was still running and he started to motor before I'd got settled. He introduced us with a wave of his hand as we were going along.

"You've got a nice house," Mary said, "and a lovely garden."

"It's alright," I mumbled, thinking that it was an odd thing to say. Some of my friends had houses that were a lot smarter than ours. Matthew had a swimming pool in his back garden.

We didn't talk very much. I think Mr Smithers had a flat tyre but he didn't seem to notice. Mary was bouncing up and down on the back seat as we made our way into the wood. We climbed out when we got to the end of the ride and Mr Smithers suggested that I took Mary on and showed her where the nest was because he wanted to see Charles.

When the Mini turned and bounced its way back to the track, I told Mary to come on but she didn't seem to want to move. I wondered if she was a bit strange in the head because she didn't seem to hear me. She stood there looking up at the sky and the trees and the undergrowth. Then she said, "Listen to the silence."

I thought she was nuts. How can you listen to silence but then she went on to explain. She lived near a main road and there was noise all the time, even during the night. To listen and only hear silence was a wonderful experience for her. She would have just stood there listening to silence if I hadn't hurried her up. I wanted to get up to where the birds had nested and see if there was any sign of them.

But there was no sign of the hobbies. We waited under the shelter of a chestnut tree. It was the time in the evening when we should have seen or heard them. The silence and stillness of the woods extended to the area around the nest. There wasn't even any sign of the second fledgling peeping over or balancing on the rim. I wondered if it was alright so I told Mary that I was going to climb the tree to look in the nest. She came too. She gave me a leg up first and then she jumped up, caught hold of the lowest branch and swung herself up like a monkey and was following me up through the branches.

The nest was empty. I looked down into it and didn't believe that the second chick had flown. He must have been at least five days younger than his sister. He wouldn't have been ready to fly. It was at this point that we heard the Mini backfiring along the ride. We slithered and slid down to the ground and I greeted Mr Smithers with the news that the younger fledgling had disappeared. He didn't seem concerned.

"He was ready to fly," he said, "he would have followed his sister."

I don't know why we had decided that the elder one was a female and the younger, a male. I suppose it was because of the difference in size. The older bird was definitely larger and female birds are generally about a third bigger and heavier than the males.

Mr Smithers said that they wouldn't be far away and would probably return to the nest each night for a while. We waited there for ages and we didn't see sight or sound of them. Mary was disappointed especially as Mr Smithers said that he was so busy marking exams that he was pretty tied up for the next few weeks and he would have to rely on us to tell him how the hobbies were getting on because he wouldn't be able to come down so often.

I told Mary that if she liked she could cycle down to the woods with me and Mr Smithers said that she could borrow his bike as long as she didn't mind cleaning it up a bit.

It was the third time that we cycled down to the woods that Mary saw the hobbies for the first time. I heard them calling first and we crunched our way through the undergrowth towards the sound. Although we could hear them, we couldn't see them. We went a bit further so that we were in the ride that was parallel to the one in which they had nested. We were only there a matter of seconds when we saw the hen bird dive out of the sky and fly from one end of the ride to the other, hardly moving her wings.

She was carried forward by the speed of her flight and the two young birds followed calling out with their immature cries. Then they were gone. We waited for ages in case they returned but they didn't. They might have come back if Mary had stayed still but she wanted to look at everything, the wild flowers, the sun's rays shining through the leaves, the patterns of the bark on the trees.

I'd never met anyone like Mary. You would be talking about something and she'd suddenly switch to a completely different subject. She did that day.

"Isn't the grass beautiful?" she said.

Grass! Grass was something to play football on. There was nothing beautiful or interesting about grass but there was the way Mary saw it. She pointed out the varieties that grew along the ride and the delicate flowers they bore and the way they swayed in the slight breeze so that they looked like waves flowing before they crashed on to the shore.

Then she stood up, turned to me and said, "Let's go for a run. We'll go to the end of this ride, along and down the next one and back here and, if we see the hobbies, we'll stop straight away."

I didn't take to that idea at all but she had already taken off and I wasn't going to let a girl beat me so I ran after her and I couldn't keep up. We ran along the route she had suggested but when she emerged from the main ride, she suddenly stopped. Two buzzards were circling lazily overhead, wings outstretched against a clear, blue sky.

"God," she said, "this is a magic place."

She threw herself down and lay on her back on the ground and gazed at the two birds floating effortlessly above us. Then they found a thermal of air and were slowly lifted higher and higher until they were little more than specks in the sky.

Mary sat up and hugged her knees close to her body and I looked at the sunlight shining on her head and thought that she wasn't bad for a girl even if she could run faster than I could and was the year above me at school.

"How do you know Mr Smithers?" I asked her.

"My mother does for him," she said.

I looked at her. Mary must have seen the expression on my face because she started to laugh. She laughed until the tears ran down her face. She kept trying to tell me something but she was laughing too much for the words to come out. I couldn't help laughing too although I had no idea what I was laughing at. Then she took a deep breath and managed to get out that her Mother didn't do for him like that. She did his housework.

"Oh," I said and I suppose there was something funny in the way I spoke because that set her off laughing again.

"You are funny, Seth," Mary said. "Come on, I'll race you back," and she'd sprung to her feet and set off before I had time to stand up. By the time I caught up with her, she was leaning against a tree trunk and looked as if she'd been waiting for ages.

"Mary," I said, throwing myself down on the ground beside her, "why doesn't his wife do the housework?"

"He hasn't got a wife. She was killed in a car crash and so was their little girl. Didn't you know? I think that's why he's so kind to Mum and me."

I hadn't known that. Somehow you don't think of teachers having private lives. I'd got to know Mr Smithers that summer but I didn't know anything about him. I thought about him for a bit and what it must be like to lose your family in an accident like that.

"What about your father. Doesn't he mind?"

"Haven't got a father," Mary said, "never had one."

"You must have had a father. It isn't biologically possible to exist without a father."

"Oh that," said Mary scornfully. "sex. Sure, I had a father in that sense but he wasn't any use to Mum or me. He was in the same class as Mum at school and he got her pregnant. As soon as he knew there was a baby on the way, he went off with another girl and got her pregnant too. She had an abortion but my mother wouldn't consider it so she got stuck with me. She left school to look after me. It meant that she couldn't go to College or get a career. She's given up a lot for me but I'll pay her back. I'll get a job and we're both going to evening classes and we'll get our A levels that way."

"Aren't you going on to college?"

"I can't can I? College costs and I can't put my mother through that. It's about time she had a life of her own."

"Don't you want to go to College?"

"Of course I do. I'd love to be a botanist and learn about plants but perhaps they mean more to me because we haven't got a garden. Still we have to be practical. Come on, Seth, we'd better be getting back. My Mum worries like crazy if I'm late."

I got up early the next morning and went for a run. Dad hadn't left for work and he seemed surprised to see me. He's generally gone to work before I appear. He didn't say anything except to tell me that Mum was down the garden checking on a bird that had come in the night before and Sophie was down there helping.

"I'm going for a run," I said.

"At seven o'clock in the morning?"

"I'm in training," I told him and set off.

I jogged down to the river. I'd planned to run along the bank but the early morning sun glinting on the water and the willows lining the opposite bank was so peaceful that I sat down and started to think, think about what Mary had told me the evening before. I had a garden and a father. All my friends did although Tom's parents were divorced but he still knew his father. He said he hated him for what he had done to his mother but he still went to stay with him every other weekend and in school holidays which meant he got left out of a lot of things. All my friends had houses with gardens. Matthew had a swimming pool in his and Jason had a paddock with ponies in it at the back of his because his kid sister liked riding. And I was going to go on to University. I hadn't thought about doing anything else. I'd never equated these things with money and, I suppose, privelege.

I missed the school bus. Mum had left a note saying that she couldn't wait any longer or she would be late for work. I would have to go to school on my bike and I was to phone her and let her know that I had arrived safely. Cycling the seven miles into school gave me some more time to think. The picture Mary had painted of her home life had disturbed me. I'd never thought about how other people lived. I'd only thought about myself and my family. By the time I reached school, I was beginning to wonder if it was me that was the odd one out, not Mary. I looked at the others in assembly that morning and wondered if I had more than they did.

We had football practice that day. I know it was the middle of summer but I still liked football better than anything else. There was a lad from Year 7 that used to turn out with us. There wasn't a lot of him. We used to call him Shrimp. He could dribble the ball up the pitch faster than any of us and we let him play in our team. He always played in his trainers and he didn't wear football colours like we did. We happened to sit down next to each other in the changing room and I noticed that he'd got a hole in his socks. I don't think I would have given it a thought before but, now, I wondered if he came from a similar background to Mary.

"Look, Shrimp," I said, "I'm throwing out last year's football kit. It's too small for me. Would it be any use to you?

"I don't know," he said.

"I don't want any money for it."

"I'll have to ask me Dad."

"It's a gift."

"Me Dad's funny about that sort of thing. He doesn't like me taking charity."

"It's not charity. It's giving you something I don't want but if it makes him feel any better, I'll charge you for it."

"How much?"

"A pound," I said. "I'll bring it in tomorrow and you can take it home and see if it fits you," and that is what I did.

He didn't even say thank you when I gave it to him but stuffed it down into his bag. When I got to school the next morning, Shrimp was standing on the pavement waiting for me.

"Me Dad said that stuff's too good for one pound. I can have it for one pound fifty," and he started to count out the money into the palm of my hand in ten and twenty pence coins. Then he turned and walked away.

I felt let down. He hadn't even said thank you. I was standing there with the money in my hands when Matthew caught up with me.

"Collecting money?" he asked, and I told him about the football kit.

"You're a fool," he said. "I advertised my old boots on the internet and I got fifty pounds for them."

I met Mary as she was coming out of the music room at the end of the morning. The others were in a rush to get down to the canteen and we had the corridor to ourselves and I told her about Shrimp and the football kit.

"That was nice of you, Seth," she said. "I know Shrimp. His name's Terence. His mother's an invalid. She's got M.S. and his father's given up work to look after her. They're nice people and, as for your friend Matthew, well there's a lot of people like that, the sort of people who have got enough but always want more."

I didn't know what MS was but I guessed it must have been something serious if Shrimp's father had to give up work to look after his mother. I asked Mum about it when I got home and she said, "Don't you remember the vicar's wife. She died last year. She had MS, multiple sclerosis it stands for. It's a horrible thing. They're doing a lot of research on it but they don't really know the cause of it. It affects the nerve ends and gradually gets into the whole body although it can go into remission for a while. The first sign that the vicar's wife had that anything was wrong was when she got this tingling in her hands and feet. Then it gradually spread over her whole body. Her brain was alright though. She knew exactly what was happening but there's no cure and there was nothing we could do to help.

I could remember the vicar's wife but I'd never thought of her as a person. I had only ever seen her in a wheel chair and she used to make funny sounds out of the side of her mouth and dribble and the vicar used to try and give her drinks through a wide straw and she couldn't swallow it properly and the liquid ran out of the side of her mouth and down her neck. And then I thought of Shrimp. Was his mother like that? I would have to ask Mary. I went and stood at the window and looked down the garden. Mum was going down the path carrying a bucket of water and I looked at her very carefully to make sure that she was walking alright and I suddenly felt very sorry for Shrimp. What would I ever do if my mother was ill? What would I do if she had MS? I shut my eyes. I couldn't bear to think about it.

I cycled down to the woods on my own on Saturday. I didn't tell Mary I was going but she couldn't have come anyway. She was at an athletics meeting with her club. She was into athletics which was why she was always running or jumping or standing on her hands and doing a double

53

somersault. I thought I was mega fit with all the football I played but I couldn't keep up with her. But this day, I wanted to be on my own. I wanted to think about things and the peace and quiet of the place was ideal for me to sort them in my own mind. The knowledge that the hobbies shared that world gave me an added strength, a kind of mental satisfaction.

I didn't say anything to Mary but she was one of the things I wanted to think about. My life had been very comfortable until I met her. I suppose I'd been sheltered from things. I had a Dad and he had a good job. Mary didn't. I felt sad for her that she couldn't go on to University and do the things she wanted. She loved the world of the hobbies and the woods and the countryside. It didn't seem right for me to think about going to College when there were people like Mary who couldn't. She knew so much about plants already and she would make a good botanist. Then I began to wonder if I wouldn't like to be a botanist too or a zoologist. I'd like to know more about birds like the hobbies. I really wanted to be a footballer but perhaps I could do something else as well.

Then there was Shrimp. Whatever was his life like with a sick mother and a father who couldn't go to work? Was there enough money to buy food? Was that why he was so small because he didn't have enough to eat? He was in the same year as Sophie and she was going to Switzerland with the school and it was going to cost four hundred pounds. I bet Shrimp wasn't going. If he couldn't find enough money to buy a pair of football boots, he wouldn't be able to afford four hundred pounds to go on a school trip. If I had four hundred pounds, I would pay for him to go I thought. But then I knew he wouldn't take it. He wouldn't even let me give him my old football kit.

Then I thought about Mr Smithers. He was O.K. but I hadn't thought that at first. I suppose Mary telling me about the car crash that had killed his wife and daughter made me look at him sort of differently. God, how would I feel if my family were killed in an accident like that? I hated getting home when everyone was out and the house was empty. How would I manage if they never came back?

I lay on my back under the huge ash tree where Mary and I used to sit and watch the hobbies hunting and flying along the ride but there was no sign of them that afternoon but there was the peace and silence that Mary loved to listen to. And I thought. I thought about the hobbies and the wonders of the countryside and I thought about this whole new world I was discovering and all because of the afternoon I had cycled down to see Charles.

The next few weeks were magic, magic for me because we were able to see the young hobbies growing into maturity, to watch them flying and hunting with their parents and, for Mary, because she was in the environment that she loved.

We didn't always see the hobbies. Sometimes the woods were dark and silent and brooding and nothing moved. Sometimes we would hear the birds' distinctive call and spend ages trying to find out where the sound was coming from. Then there would be the times when we came across them unexpectedly and froze on the spot so that our movement didn't disturb them. Their favourite hunting ground was the ride that ran parallel to the one in which they had nested. The times that I loved to see them most was when they rose high in the air hawking the insects that were rising above the tree tops in the early evening. Then they would be airborne until the sun began to set. We would watch them soaring and stooping in the fading light until they became dark silhouettes against the setting sun.

There was one evening that I will never forget. Mary and I had cycled down to the woods straight after school. Mum had made sandwiches for us both. We had found a good place beneath the ash tree for our picnic. It was at the end of the ride where we often saw the hobbies hunting but, that evening, there wasn't sight or sound of them. Mary lay back on the ground and talked in her lazy voice about the patterns the leaves were making against the sky looking like lace when I noticed the moths. At first there were only a few brown hawk moths fluttering along the ride, weaving erratic patterns against the undergrowth. Mary sat up when I pointed them out. Then their numbers increased and they were drawn upwards in a vibrating column. There were enough of them to cast an elongated shadow on the ground which changed shape and direction as their numbers multiplied.

"They're hatching out," Mary said, "I read about it in a book but I've never seen it happen before."

As far as we could see along the ride, there were other miniature columns lifting into the air as the moths escaped from their chrysalli.

We watched the moths as they left the bulk of the vibrating column and fluttered haphazardly along the ride. Then the hobbies arrived. At first they flew straight through the moths at a terrific speed, scattering them with the disturbance of the air that their flight had caused. Then they turned and swung in towards the column of emerging moths and there was menace and determination in their flight. They swooped on to the luckless insects seizing them as they flew, reaching out and grabbing them, one after the other, with their talons. They tore the wings from each one and swallowed the body, immediately plucking another from the air and treating it in the same way. They gorged themselves on the moths, eating them until their crops stood out like boils on their necks and still they flew amongst their prey. At first the adult birds flew alone but then, with that distinctive cry of the young birds, the other two joined them, flying and killing and devouring the moths without pausing in their flight. We sat there watching as the moths flew their erratic flight towards the shelter of the trees and there were no more torn wings fluttering towards the ground like tarnished snowflakes and the call of the tawny owls told of the approaching night.

We never saw the four birds flying together again.

Then it was all over.

It was August the ninth. I can remember the date clearly because that was Gran's birthday and I'd just put the phone down from talking to her when there was a squeal of brakes and a clanging sound as something hit the gates and I knew that Rex had arrived.

"The swifts are on the move," he called out when he saw me. "Charlie's phoned up and said they're going over in there thousands. Come on."

I shouted down the garden to Mum to tell her where I was going and jumped into the Mini. Mary was already tucked into the back seat amongst all the debris.

You could never have claimed that Rex drove slowly but he must have exceeded the speed limit ten times over that evening. Mary was bouncing up and down like a rubber ball much too violently to talk although we did have a kind of jerky conversation, mostly starting sentences and being unable to finish them.

Rex came to a stop at the bottom of the hill that overlooked the lake where Mum had released the kingfisher. The wood was behind us but we hardly looked at it because flying overhead were the swifts, thousands and thousands of them. Charlie and Judy were already standing on the hill watching along with Clarence and Albert alongside them. Charlie said that they had started flying over in the afternoon, about half past four when he was returning from the breeding pens. There had been a trickle of the birds at first but then more and more had appeared all flying in the same direction until they darkened the sky.

"I've seen swifts leaving before," Charles said, "but never like this."

Rex had brought two pairs of binoculars and handed them to Mary and me but we didn't need them. There were so many birds that they seemed to fill the universe.

"The last of the summer birds to come and the first to leave," Charles muttered.

"Does that mean the hobbies are going too?" I asked.

"They might," Rex said, "even if they don't fly with the swifts they won't be long following them."

I felt sad. I didn't want them to go. I wanted that summer to go on for ever.

The swifts were flying towards the lake in streams. They converged over the water and became a river that flew steadily south westwards across the sky. And they never stopped. The flow was continuous. If anything, it increased in density. The birds approached the lake from three different directions, merging and flowing on without a pause. We stood there and watched, hypnotised by the sight and power of their flight, completely silenced by the magnitude of it all. I thought back to the single group that Charles and I had seen four months earlier when the hobby had dived through the small cloud of birds and compared them to this continuous flow of living creatures. We were seeing one of the wonders of nature and I suddenly felt insignificant and everything that I thought was important like my team winning the football tournament didn't seem to matter quite so much. I spoke about it to Mary some time later and she said she had felt the same. She had felt overwhelmed.

And the swifts kept coming, a steady stream of them. I lifted the binoculars to my eyes and saw that there were more swifts above the layer that we were watching and more above them. They were reaching up towards the heavens. They were filling the universe. I couldn't believe there were so many swifts in the world. I know Id been watching the hobbies but I'd been keeping my eyes on the swifts as well. We hadn't a single pair nesting in the village and we only found three nesting pairs in Bentworth and now there were thousands and thousands of them flying over our heads.

Judy and Mary went down to the cottage to make some sandwiches and a flask of tea. When they returned, we sat on the grass and ate and watched. We didn't talk. There was nothing we could say. We were all mesmerized by the river of birds flowing above us. As the sun set we saw the swifts as a moving frieze of black arrows against a darkening sky and, at some time, the two adult hobbies must have lifted into the air and flown south with them. The two young birds were left behind.

It was two days later that I cycled down to the plantation and walked round with Charles. It didn't seem the same without the hobbies. I felt their absence and I missed them. As we came level with the fir tree, something made me look up and there were the two young hobbies sitting on the branch where they had stood before they made their first flights. They seemed to look down at us as if they were thinking, "Who are these strange creatures trespassing in our territory?" They looked as complete and as confident as their parents had looked when I had first seen them.

The two fledglings chose that moment to take to the air and fly along the ride and up and over the young trees at the end.

"I wondered if that would happen," Charles said. "They'll follow on as soon as their flight is stronger."

We never saw them again. Mary came down with me several times and we walked right round the woods but the nights were beginning to draw in and the hobbies had flown. The woods seemed so empty without them but Mary soon found other things that interested her, the young green woodpeckers with their raucous laugh disturbing the silence and the buzzards soaring effortlessly above our heads, the grasshoppers landing on our trainers and the berries and seeds along the hedgerows. One evening we went out with Charles badger watching. Another time, we got up early and went down to hear the dawn chorus. Sometimes David came with us but none of the rest of the gang wanted to join us. They liked playing football best and they thought that watching birds was boring.

Then it was the end of the summer holidays and time to get ready for school. I was sorting out my things when Mary came round, on Rex's old bike which was far too big and heavy for her, and said, "Let's go for a walk. I've got something special to tell you."

I could see that she was excited. Her face was flushed and she couldn't stop smiling, so I pushed everything to one side and followed her down the lane. We walked down towards the river but Mary couldn't wait to tell me her secret.

"I'm going to be a bridesmaid," she said.

"Is that it? Is that the special something?"

I wasn't in to bridesmaids.

"Well, aren't you going to ask me who is getting married?"

"Well, who is?"

"My mother. Isn't it wonderful? Aren't you going to ask who she's marrying?"

"Who is she marrying?" I asked. I wasn't really interested.

"Rex," she said. "Rex is going to be my stepfather. But you're not to tell anyone, Seth. Promise. They don't want anyone to know. They don't want any fuss but I had to tell someone and Rex said that I can tell you. I can't keep it all to myself."

I didn't know what to say. I'd never thought about teachers falling in love and getting married and that sort of thing. Mary was still prattling on, telling me how Rex had said that he would like her to stay on at school and go to University and he had explained to her how he had come to look on her as a daughter although she could never be the little girl that had been killed in the accident. She could never take her place but she would still be his daughter.

"Wasn't that a lovely thing for him to say?" she said.

I muttered something but I don't think she heard. She was going on and on. I had never seen anyone so excited. Then she started doing cartwheels along the river bank and I caught hold of her because I thought she was going to fall in and tried to get her to sit down. She did after a while. I had never seen her like this in fact I'd never seen anyone like Mary was that afternoon. She couldn't talk about anything else.

"Rex said that he would adopt me if that's what I would like and I could have the same surname. Mary Smithers sounds sort of right doesn't it? Perhaps I will but Rex said that I mustn't decide in a hurry. What do you think, Seth? What would you do? Jones is alright but it's kind of ordinary." She chattered on and on like that all the way back to our house and didn't give me a chance to answer any of the questions she was throwing at me.

I stood at our gate as Mary picked up her bike and started off. She wobbled for a bit, then stopped and looked over her shoulder back at me. "Oh Seth, I'm so happy," and she got back on her bike and pedalled down the lane as if she was driving in the Grand Prix.

"Wasn't that Mary with you?" Mum asked when I went in. "Doesn't she want to stay for tea?"

"She's got other things to do," I said.

Mum looked at me a bit straight. I think she thought we'd had a row or something like that. You can't hide much from my mother.

I would have liked to tell Mum and Dad about Rex getting married but Mary had sworn me to secrecy so I kept quiet but I did think I ought to get him a present. A wedding is sort of special. I thought about it a lot and decided that I would paint a picture of a hobby and give him that. So I started going to the art room in the lunch hour when we weren't playing football. I wanted my picture to be special. I got the ride and the trees sketched in but, somehow, the hobby I painted didn't come right. I was sitting there looking at what I had done when the art teacher came in and, drawing up a chair, he sat down beside me and commented on what I had drawn.

"The bird isn't right," I told him.

"It looks fine to me," he said.

"No," I said, "the wings aren't right. This is special and it's got to be right. I want to give it to Mr Smithers for his wedding present."

"What?"

The explosion of sound startled me and I realised I'd blown it. I hadn't told a soul about Mary's mother and Mr Smithers getting married and then it had slipped out. The art master said he would keep it to himself when I explained things to him but I didn't believe him. He had the look on his face that people have when they make a promise but keep their fingers crossed behind their backs which means there'll be nothing wrong if they break it. All the same I was relieved when half term came and the news of the wedding hadn't got round the school. I thought I'd go and thank the art teacher when it was all over.

The wedding was on the Saturday. Judy and Charles were there and so was our family. It turned out that we all knew about it and hadn't discussed it because we didn't think anyone else knew.

Mr Smither's sister had come up from Wales. I knew then why Mr Smithers spoke in such a loud voice. It was to make himself heard above his sister's. She never stopped talking. The words just tumbled out of her mouth in a sing song kind of way so that you really had to concentrate to make out what she meant. And once she started, she didn't stop. The usher had to ask her to be quiet so that the ceremony could start.

I'd never met Mary's mother before but I felt I knew her because she looked like Mary. She had the same fair hair and the same smiley face. Mary looked good. She wore a cream dress and she carried a bouquet of cream and mauve flowers. Her hair was loose over her shoulders and she wasn't wearing glasses.

"Rex bought me contact lenses," she whispered to me as we went in, "do they look alright."

That was about the stupidest thing she could have asked. How could I tell her what her contact lenses looked like? You couldn't see them when she had them in. I didn't tell her that though. I told her that she looked brill and she did. So did her mother. She wore a cream suit with a corsage of flowers that matched Mary's bouquet. They looked more like sisters than mother and daughter. As for Rex, I had never seen him looking so smart. I'd got used to seeing him in his shorts and bobble hat, so it was a shock to see him in a fawn suit, cream shirt and brown tie. And they were so happy. The three of them didn't stop smiling and neither did we.

I'd never been to a wedding before and I didn't know what to expect. It was only a short ceremony. Then they signed the register and Rex took an awful long time kissing the bride. We were all going back to Charles and Judy's for lunch and then Rex and Claire were going away for a few days. Mary was going to stay with Charles and Judy.

It was so quiet in the Registry Office that the shout that greeted the couple as they went out of the front door was a terrific shock. It even silenced Rex's sister. We wondered whatever was happening. Then the roar of Rex's laughter and Claire's giggling added to the noise. I pushed my way out beside them and I reckoned half the school had turned out. They'd even strung streamers between the lamp posts. Broad Street was lined with cheering students and they all started to move up towards the town hall. They completely blocked the road. Cars started to hoot, trying to push their way through.

Then I saw our two P.E. teachers and the Art teacher and they were grinning all over their faces. They cleared a path through the crowd and an old fashioned cream Rolls Royce came through and stopped in front of Rex and Claire. It was decorated with ribbons and lots of tin cans were tied on the back of it. The Art teacher opened the door with a flourish and invited Rex and Claire into it. They weren't driven away, they were pulled. Two ropes were fixed to the front of the car and the teachers and lots of students pulled it up the hill to the school. People were waiting in the hall and they clapped when we all went in. There was champagne and biscuits and canapes.

"I don't know," Rex's voice boomed out. "You can't keep anything quiet in Alresford."

Everyone laughed and the Art teacher looked across at me and winked.

Then the headmaster motioned everyone to be quiet and told Rex and Claire that they had all wanted to share this moment with them. He went on to say that they had both had to face more trauma and difficulties than most people had to face during the whole of their lives but those times were behind them now and they all wished them every happiness in their new lives. Then he gave Rex an envelope and said he hoped that he would accept it along with their sincere, good wishes.

Rex took the envelope. He cleared his throat several times as if he was going to say something but no words came. He seemed to be overcome with emotion and there was an awkward few seconds. Nobody had ever seen Rex speechless. The P.E. teacher saved the day by calling for three cheers. I don't think anyone could have shouted louder and, as the sound of the last cheer died down, we could hear the students who were still waiting outside cheering and clapping as well.

Mary was crying. Tears were running down her face. "What's the matter," I asked her.

"I'm so happy," she said but she still went on sobbing.

I wondered if I should put my arm round her to comfort her but Judy saved the day. She came across and gave her a big hug. I don't think she was far off tears herself and I thought weddings were supposed to be happy.

We didn't get back to Charles and Judy's until nearly four o'clock. Judy worried that the joint of beef she had left in the Aga would be overcooked but nobody would have minded if it had been. We were a bit squashed round their dining table but it didn't matter. Nothing mattered that day.

I wondered when I should give Rex my present. I'd put it in a frame but it still looked kind of ordinary. You could see the fir tree clearly enough and a corner of the nest with one of the fledglings standing on the branch beside it and there was the male hobby flying in towards the nest. I had to paint him in at the top of the picture because I had wanted to show his silhouette against the sky. Down in the other corner, I had painted Rex wearing his red bobble hat and knee length shorts. He was standing in front of his Mini.

I hid my parcel in the hedge waiting until I could get Rex on his own. I didn't think that was ever going to be. Judy hadn't only cooked the beef and all the trimmings, she must have made all the puddings in the cookery book. We had trifles and jellies and meringues. We even had Christmas pudding and Judy kept saying that she didn't want anything left.

Then Rex announced that he needed a breath of fresh air and the others started to clear the table before Judy brought on the wedding cake.

"I need a break too," I said with feeling and I followed Rex out.

He was standing, looking out over the lake. I don't think he even noticed me. I retrieved the picture and gave it to him.

"What's this?" he asked.

"It's for you," I said.

I didn't think he liked it when he unwrapped the picture. He stood there staring at it and I began to wish that I hadn't painted it. He was holding it in front of him but he seemed to be looking beyond it as if he was staring at something on the horizon. Then he looked at me and smiled.

"It's great, Seth," he said. "I'm going to hang it in pride of place in our house," and he stood there staring at it. "It's been a wonderful summer, hasn't it, and I think those birds have changed our lives in a way. Seeing them fly and bring up their young has given me a sense of peace and made me put my own life and feelings in perspective, made me think of what really matters in life. It's been a good year."

"Yes," I said, "it has. It's been the year of the hobbies."